For M., L., and H., with love   ~ G. W.

For Beatrice   ~ P. H.

Text copyright © 2004 by Gina Wilson
Illustrations copyright © 2004 by Paul Howard

First U.S. edition 2004

Library of Congress Cataloging-in-Publication Data is available.

Library of Congress Catalog Card Number 2003069561

ISBN 0-7636-2518-3

2 4 6 8 10 9 7 5 3 1

Printed in China

This book was typeset in Kabel Book.
The illustrations were done in pencil, watercolor, and crayon.

Candlewick Press
2067 Massachusetts Avenue
Cambridge, Massachusetts 02140

visit us at www.candlewick.com

GRANDMA'S BEARS

Gina Wilson

illustrated by
Paul Howard

CANDLEWICK PRESS
CAMBRIDGE, MASSACHUSETTS

Nat's grandma shared her cottage with bears. Whenever Nat came to supper, the bears hid themselves away, but this time he was staying the whole night.

"So I'll see them now, won't I?" he said, tramping home along the lane with Grandma. "Are they big?"

"Quite big," said Grandma.

"And fierce?"

"Not when I'm around."

"Will they like me?"

"They will, if you like them."

"I'll love them," said Nat.

But when Grandma pushed open the front door, Nat suddenly wasn't so sure. The way was blocked by a bear, who seemed very unhappy. He was groaning loudly and holding his head in his paws.

"Poor Arthur!" sighed Grandma.
"He hates rain and mess.
He likes things tidy.
Let's shake our coats outside."

"Let's leave our boots on the mat," whispered Nat.

"Good idea. And you can teach him one of your clever games while I put the kettle on."

Nat found himself alone in the hallway with Arthur. He looked up at him nervously, and Arthur blinked down.

"Try this," said Nat. He started slowly hopping from square to square on the tiled floor, first black, then white. Arthur followed him, **splodge, splodge,** on one enormous leather-padded paw.

"Out!" shouted Nat.
"You're stepping on
the lines!
Let's try again."

When the game was over,
Arthur combed his own hair,
then Nat's, with his long,
delicate claws. He'd forgotten
about the rain.

Grandma was in the kitchen with a round woolly bear called Aggie. Aggie was leaning over the sink, rubbing her eyes. "She got soap in them," explained Grandma.

Aggie turned around. She couldn't see well. Her nose was frothy with suds. "She thought it was ice cream," said Grandma.

Nat wanted to give Aggie a hug, but he didn't dare. "Can we find her a treat?" he asked.

"Doughnuts?" suggested Grandma. "I bought some for our snack. You hand them out while I go and light the fire."

Nat sat at the table and helped himself. "Want one, Aggie?"

She bounded forward, friendly and wet. **SCHLOMPFFF!** She was in the mood to polish them all off at once. "Slow down!" giggled Nat. "One for you, one for me . . . "

When the doughnuts were finished, Aggie slurped the sugar and jam off her own nose, then Nat's, with her flannelly tongue. She'd forgotten about the soapsuds.

The living room was warm. Grandma
had lit the fire and turned on the news.
"That'll be Mommy," she said as the
phone started ringing in the hall.

"Tell her I can't talk," said Nat.
"I'm too busy with the bears!"

He could see Tumtum, sprawling crossly
under the table with his eyes shut.

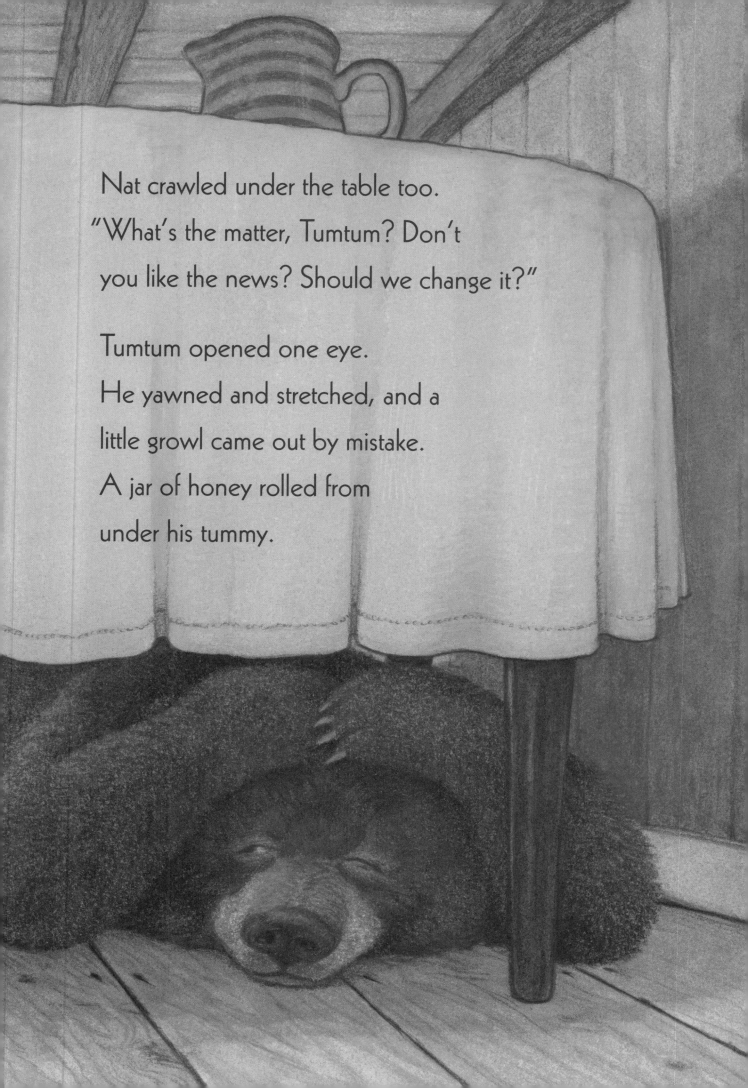

Nat crawled under the table too. "What's the matter, Tumtum? Don't you like the news? Should we change it?"

Tumtum opened one eye. He yawned and stretched, and a little growl came out by mistake. A jar of honey rolled from under his tummy.

He padded across to the
TV and walloped its buttons.

"Football!" cheered Grandma,
coming in with supper on
a tray. "Wow!"

When it was bedtime,
Nat peered up Grandma's
twisty staircase. He shivered.
"It's scary up there.
Can the bears come too?"

"There might be more bears upstairs,"
said Grandma, taking his hand.

And there, in the bathroom, was
shaggy old Floss! She loomed in the
steam like a huge, snowy bath towel.
It was all her own fur. When Nat
got out of the bath, she
wrapped herself
tightly round him.

Grandma tucked Nat into bed
and settled down to read his
favorite story.

All the bears came padding
in to listen.

Arthur stood on one leg, practicing his balancing.

Aggie and Tumtum jumped up on the bed for cuddles.

Floss lay at Grandma's feet, gazing up proudly at the
most spotless boy ever to come out of her bathroom.

"Sleep tight, Nat," said Grandma at
the end of the story. She kissed him.
"Thank you for loving my bears."

"I knew I would," said Nat.
"Can they stay with me? It's dark."

Grandma shook her head. "You'll be all right."
She gave him another kiss. "Just snuggle
right down." She went away, and her bears
went with her, leaving only a night-light
to keep Nat company.

Then Nat was frightened. He was all alone.
The shadows grew bigger and darker.
They crept closer. He dived deep down
under the blankets and pulled them over his head.

Then, as he was holding his breath and
snuggling right down as Grandma had said,
he suddenly felt his feet sinking into
something warm and furry.

The something started licking
his toes. It gave a tiny grunt
and came snuffling up to see
who the toes belonged to.

"Oh!" gasped Nat.
He was face to face with
a smoky gray bear cub,
Grandma's littlest of all,
with round brown eyes
and a nosy nose.

Smoky wasn't at all afraid of
shadows. He liked tummy tickles
and big hugs. He wanted to lie
with his head on the pillow
beside Nat's.

"Should we close our eyes now?"
yawned Nat. He'd forgotten
about the shadows.

At midnight, Grandma looked in and found them both fast asleep. "Dear Smoky!" she whispered.

"Thank you for loving my Nat!"
She left them to sleep there all night.